1987

To Gayle,
with love!

THE BAD DREAM

Jim Aylesworth

Illustrations by Judith Friedman

Albert Whitman & Company, Niles, Illinois

Text © 1985 by Jim Aylesworth
Illustrations © 1985 by Judith Friedman
Published in 1985 by Albert Whitman & Company, Niles, Illinois
Published simultaneously in Canada by General Publishing, Limited, Toronto.
10 9 8 7 6 5 4 3 2

Library of Congress Cataloging in Publication Data

Aylesworth, Jim.
    The bad dream.

    Summary: When a little boy is awakened by a bad
dream, his parents comfort him by reminding him that
nightmares are not real.
    1. Children's stories, American. [1. Nightmares—
Fiction. 2. Dreams—Fiction. 3. Sleep—Fiction]
I. Friedman, Judith, 1945—ill. II. Title.
PZ7.A983Bad 1985   [E]   85-685
ISBN 0-8075-0506-4

To Momma Maggie   J. A.
To David   J. F.

It was late. The little house was dark, and all was quiet.

Inside, moonlight shone in crooked squares
across the floor. And every hour, the clock
in the corner gently chimed away the night,
ding dong   *ding dong*
ding dong
ding dong.

Down the hall, a mother and a father lay sleeping, side by side. And just across the way, their little boy lay dreaming.

In the dream, the boy and his friends were walking home from school. The afternoon sun shone brightly, and the trees were filled with yellow leaves.

Then, they were playing in the park, laughing and running and swinging and sliding.

Suddenly, strangely, the friends were gone, and the little boy was alone. He had played too long. The sun was going down. His mother would be worried.

"I'm late!" said the boy, and he began to run.
But as he ran, the sidewalk grew longer and
longer. His legs felt heavier and heavier.
The faster he tried to run, the slower
he went.

Then he was in the alley, near the yard with the bad dog. The gate was open, and the dog was running toward him,

                                                                 barking,

                                                                                 barking,

                                                                                       barking.

In fear, the boy began to climb the alley fence,
higher and higher. Closer and closer came the
dog. Louder and louder he barked.

Rrroof!

Woof   Woof   Woof

Rrrroof!

Rrrroof!

Then the boy slipped
and fell,

down,
down,
down.

"Mommy! Mommy!"

Bump.

He fell out of bed. He lay still, his heart thumping. Suddenly the room was filled with light, and his mother was standing over him. "Are you all right?" she asked.

"I was late from school!" said the boy. "And there was a bad dog, and . . ."

"Don't be afraid," said his mother. "You were having a dream. It wasn't real."

"What's going on?" asked the father. "You two having a party here in the middle of the night?"

"A bad dream," said the mother.

"Ugh!" said the father. "I hate bad dreams."

"Do you have them, too?" asked the boy.

"Everybody has bad dreams," answered the father. "But they can't hurt you. They're not real, you know."

"I know," said the boy.

"I love you," said the mother, giving the little boy a kiss.

"Me too!" said the father. "I'll see you in the morning."

"Goodnight," said the boy.

Then the mother and the father went back across the hall, and the little boy snuggled down under his covers. Soon they were all asleep.

As they slept, moonlight shone in crooked
squares across the floor, and the clock in the
corner gently chimed away the night,
ding dong   *ding dong*
ding dong
ding dong.